Ladybird books are widely available, but in case of difficulty may be ordered by post or telephone from:

Ladybird Books – Cash Sales Department Littlegate Road Paignton Devon TQ3 3BE
Telephone 01803 554761

A catalogue record for this book is available from the British Library

Published by Ladybird Books Ltd Loughborough Leicestershire UK
Ladybird Books Inc Auburn Maine 04210 USA

JASPER'S
Jungle Journey

by Val Biro

Picture
Ladybird

Jasper the little elephant had lost his
teddy bear in the jungle.

First, he searched the tall green grass.
What did he see?

A snake in coils, bright as brass!

Then, behind a twisted tree,
what did he see?

Two chimps having chips and tea!

By some rough and rugged rocks,
what did he see?

A lion, wearing purple socks!

On the bank of a reedy river,
what did he see?

A croc with a cold, all a-shiver!

In the swampy slushy ooze,
what did he see?

A hippo yawn, before his snooze!

Jasper on his search for bear,
what did he see?

A giraffe without a care!

By some trees all tossed and torn,
what did he see?

A rhino with an enormous horn!

In a stripey-shaded nook,
what did he see?

A zebra, reading a cookery book!

Searching for bear under the trees,
what did he see?

A camel wearing dungarees!

Then he got a fearful fright,
what did he see?

A roaring tiger. What a sight!

Jasper ran home. And when he got there,
what did he see?

Mum — who had found his teddy bear!

Picture Ladybird

Books for reading aloud with 2–6 year olds

The *Picture Ladybird* range is full of exciting stories and rhymes that are perfect to read aloud and share. There is something for everyone – animal stories, bedtime stories, rhyming stories – and lots more!

Ten titles for you to collect

WISHING MOON AGE 3+
written & illustrated by Lesley Harker

Persephone Brown wanted to be BIG. All she ever saw were feet and knees – it really wasn't on. Then one special night her wish came true. Persephone Brown just grew and grew and *GREW…*

DON'T WORRY WILLIAM AGE 3+
by Christine Morton
illustrated by Nigel McMullen

It's a sleepy dark night. A creepy dark night. A night for naughty bears to creep downstairs and have an adventure. But, going in search of biscuits to make them brave, Horace and William hear a bang–a very loud bang–an On-The-Stairs bang! Whatever can it be?

BENEDICT GOES TO THE BEACH AGE 3+
written & illustrated by Chris Demarest

It's hot in the city – *really* hot. Poor Benedict just *has* to cool off. There is only one thing for it, head for the beach – *any* beach! Deciding is the easy part – getting there is another matter altogether…

TOOT! LEARNS TO FLY AGE 3+
by Geraldine Taylor & Jill Harker
illustrated by Georgien Overwater

It's time for Toot to learn to fly, to try and zoom across the sky. First there's take off – watch it – steady! Whoops! Bump! He's not quite ready! Follow Toot's route across the sky and see if he ever *does* learn to fly!

JOE AND THE FARM GOOSE AGE 2+
by Geraldine Taylor & Jill Harker
illustrated by Jakki Wood

A perfect way to introduce young children to farmyard life. There is lots to see and talk about – pigs and their piglets, cows and sheep, hens in the barn – and Joe's special friend – a very inquisitive goose!

THE STAR THAT FELL AGE 3+
by Karen Hayles
illustrated by Cliff Wright

When a star falls from the night sky, Fox and all the other animals want its precious warmth and brightness. When Dog finds the star he gives it to his friend Maddy. But as Maddy's dad tells her, all stars belong to the sky, and soon she must give it back.

TELEPHONE TED AGE 3+
by Joan Stimson
illustrated by Peter Stevenson

When Charlie starts playgroup poor Ted is left sitting at home like a stuffed toy. It's not much fun being a teddy on your own with no one to talk to. But then – *brring, brring* – the telephone rings, and that's when Ted's adventure begins.

JASPER'S JUNGLE JOURNEY AGE 3+
written & illustrated by Val Biro

What's behind those rugged rocks? A lion wearing purple socks! Just one of the strange sights Jasper encounters as he goes in search of his lost teddy bear. A delightful rhyming story full of jungle surprises!

SHOO FLY SHOO! AGE 4+
by Brian Moses
illustrated by Trevor Dunton

If a fly flies by and it's bothering you, just swish it and swash it and tell it to *shoo!* Trace the trail of the buzzing, zuzzing fly in this gloriously silly rhyming story.

GOING TO PLAYGROUP AGE 2+
by Geraldine Taylor & Jill Harker
illustrated by Terry McKenna

Tom's day at playgroup is full of exciting activities. He's a cook, a mechanic, a pirate and a band leader… he even flies to the moon! Ideal for children starting playgroup and full of ideas for having fun at home, too!